GO-KART RACERS

by Jack D. Clifford

Illustrated by Russ Daff

W
FRANKLIN WATTS
LONDON • SYDNEY

Sam and Joe were playing a new game.
They were racing go-karts through
the desert.

"I've got a fuel boost!" yelled Sam.

"I've got a sand cloud!" cried Joe.

Suddenly, a red light shone …

Sam and Joe were in the desert
under the burning sun.

"Where are we?" asked Joe.

"We must be in the game!" Sam replied.

Sam and Joe raced on.

Then another go-kart sped past.

"That was Dragstar!" yelled Sam.

"We have to beat him or he'll be Desert Champion!"

Suddenly, their go-karts started to splutter. Sam and Joe slowed down near a group of drivers.

Then their go-karts stopped.

"What happened?" Sam asked.

"We ran out of fuel," said one driver.

"We're stuck," said another. "And it

looks like you are too."

"How did we all run out of fuel?"
asked Joe.

"We think Dragstar cheated and put holes in our tanks," said the drivers. "Now he'll win the whole championship – not just this race."

"No way!" said Sam. "My fuel boost will get us to the finish line."
"And my sand cloud will slow Dragstar down," said Joe.

"Take the short cut!" cried the other drivers. "That way! Hurry!"

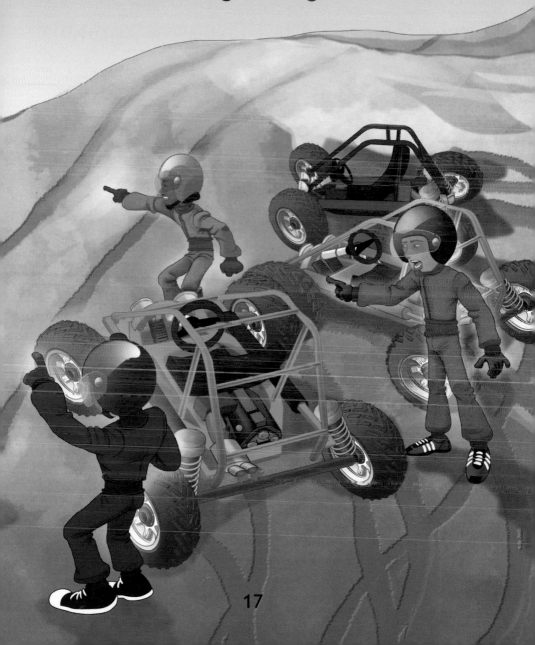

17

Joe jumped on Sam's go-kart and they sped off with the fuel boost. Before long, they could see Dragstar's go-kart.

Then they heard him laughing.

"They'll never get out of the desert

alive!" he cackled.

Sam and Joe roared up.

"Cheats don't win!" yelled Joe,

throwing his sand cloud.

Sam and Joe raced across the finish line
with Dragstar just behind them.

"Dragstar, where are the other drivers?"

shouted Joe.

"And what did you do to everyone's go-karts?" yelled Sam.

A voice announced: "And the Desert Champion is not yet decided! Dragstar, you are disqualified for cheating! Now let's find the other drivers."

Sam and Joe cheered, then a red light

shone ...

... and they were back home.

"Great game!" said Sam.

"Thirsty work!" laughed Joe.

PUZZLE TIME

Can you put these pictures

in the correct order?

Tell the story in your own words

with YOU as the hero!

TURN OVER FOR ANSWERS!

ANSWERS

The correct order is: b, a, d, c.

First published in 2011 by
Franklin Watts
338 Euston Road
London
NW1 3BH

Franklin Watts Australia
Level 17/207 Kent Street
Sydney
NSW 2000

Text © Jack D. Clifford 2011
Illustration © Russ Daff 2011

The rights of Jack D. Clifford to be
identified as the author and Russ Daff
as the illustrator of this Work have been
asserted in accordance with the Copyright,
Designs and Patents Act, 1988.

A CIP catalogue record for this book is
available from the British Library.

ISBN 978 1 4451 0308 2 (hbk)
ISBN 978 1 4451 0316 7 (pbk)

Series Editor: Jackie Hamley
Series Advisor: Catherine Glavina
Series Designer: Peter Scoulding

Printed in China

Franklin Watts is a division of Hachette Children's Books,
an Hachette UK company. www.hachette.co.uk